S0-ABP-664

Goodbye, Max

by HOLLY KELLER

GREENWILLOW BOOKS, New York

The full-color art was prepared with colored inks, dyes, and pencils and a separate black line overlay. The typeface is Korinna.

Library of Congress Cataloging-in-Publication Data
Keller, Holly.   Goodbye, Max.
Summary: Ben blames his parents for the death of his dog, Max,
and does not want the new puppy they have brought home.
[1. Death—Fiction.   2. Grief—Fiction.   3. Dogs—Fiction]
I. Title.   PZ7.K28132Go 1987   [E]   86-4680
ISBN 0-688-06561-9   ISBN 0-688-06562-7 (lib. bdg.)

FOR CAROLE AND BILL

Ben watched a red leaf fall to the ground.
It landed right near the place where Papa
had buried Max the week before.

"He was old," Papa said.

"I know," Ben answered. "But we were friends."

"A new dog can be a friend," Papa said.

Ben shook his head. "Not like Max."

When Papa brought home a puppy,
Ben didn't want to look at him.
"He's ugly," Ben said, "and he can't
do anything."

"What should we call him?" Papa asked.
"Nothing," Ben said angrily. He went to his
room and slammed the door.

Zach came over to play ball,
but Ben wouldn't come down.
"Just for a little while," Zach shouted.
Ben shut the window.

Ben stretched out on his bed and put his head under the pillow. It wasn't fair.

He thought about the day Max got sick.
He and Mama took Max to the vet.
They did everything Dr. Chase said,
but the next day Max was worse.

Ben wanted to stay home from school,
but Mama said he should go.
"You can take care of Max when you
come home," she said.

But Max died while Ben was at school.

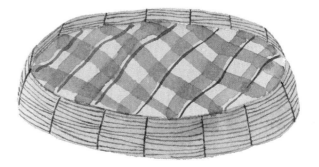

"I hate Dr. Chase," Ben shouted.

"He tried, Ben," Mama said, "but Max
was very old."

"You shouldn't have made me go to school!" Ben cried.

Mama poured Ben a glass of milk.

"There was nothing more to do," she said gently.

Ben couldn't believe that Max was dead.

Mama knocked at the door.

"Time to deliver the papers, Ben."

Ben picked up the bag of newspapers
and started down the street. Zach was
waiting at the corner to help him.

For a while they didn't talk.
Zach did one side of the street
and Ben did the other.

Finally Zach said, "Max used
to carry Mr. Brown's paper right to the door."
Ben smiled. "Remember last month when
he dropped it right in the puddle just as
Mr. Brown was about to take it?"
Zach laughed. "Yeah," he said, "I guess Max
couldn't hold it as tight as he used to."

"But that wasn't as good as the time he ate Mrs. Murphy's TV section after she scolded him for barking at her cat," Ben said, and he laughed too. "Max's eyes were so bad he probably didn't even see that dumb cat."

"Boy, I miss him," Ben said.

"Yeah," Zach said, "me too. But he was really old."

Ben didn't answer.

He sat down on the curb and started to cry.
Zach sat down next to him, and he cried too.
Ben cried until he couldn't cry anymore.

Then he wiped his eyes on his sleeve.

"Come on," Zach said.

"Let's go back to your house."

Ben stopped in the yard for a minute.

Mama was fixing dinner. "We're having hamburgers, Zach. Do you want to stay?" she asked.

"Sure," Zach said.

Ben knelt down to look at the puppy.

He picked him up.

The puppy licked Ben's face.

"Yuck," Ben said, but he was smiling.

"Did you name him yet?" Zach asked.

"No," Ben said, "but we can now."